Dear Daniel & Jayden,

It was so awesome to have you as my students this summer.

Both of you are incredibly hardworking and respectful.

I hope you can always remember the love your dad has for you.

Love,
Ms. Jung

We dedicate this book to our dad,
who has made great sacrifices
to provide and care for our family.
We love you very much.

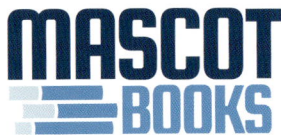

www.mascotbooks.com

Daddy's Love For Me

©2020 Sarah and JoAnn Jung. All Rights Reserved. No part of this publication may be reproduced, stored in a retrieval system or transmitted in any form by any means electronic, mechanical, or photocopying, recording or otherwise without the permission of the author.

For more information, please contact:
Mascot Books
620 Herndon Parkway, Suite 320
Herndon, VA 20170
info@mascotbooks.com

Library of Congress Control Number: 2020904170

CPSIA Code: PRTWP0720A
ISBN-13: 978-1-64543-251-7

Printed in South Korea

Daddy's Love For Me

Sarah and JoAnn Jung
Illustrated by Chiara Civati

MY DADDY LOVES ME.

But I didn't always know that.
Here is how I know now.

I used to think Daddy was stingy.

Whenever I asked him to buy me new board games and stuffed animals, he scrunched up his face and shook his head side to side. That was his way of saying, "No."

My friend Jenny has so many toys that her toy boxes overflow, but I only own two sets of board games and one teddy bear. When Jenny comes over for playdates, I'm embarrassed to take out my toys.

I used to think Daddy didn't care about me.

Whenever I got hurt, I wanted him to hug me and say, "You'll feel better soon!"

Instead, he always told me, "I'm sorry, Sumi. Daddy's tired. Why don't you go to Mommy?"

When my friend Lina gets hurt, her daddy kisses her booboos and lets her cry on his shoulder until she feels better. Not my daddy.

I used to think Daddy didn't want to see me.

He comes home from work right before my bedtime and immediately plops down on the sofa to sleep. Sometimes he snores so loudly it hurts my ears!

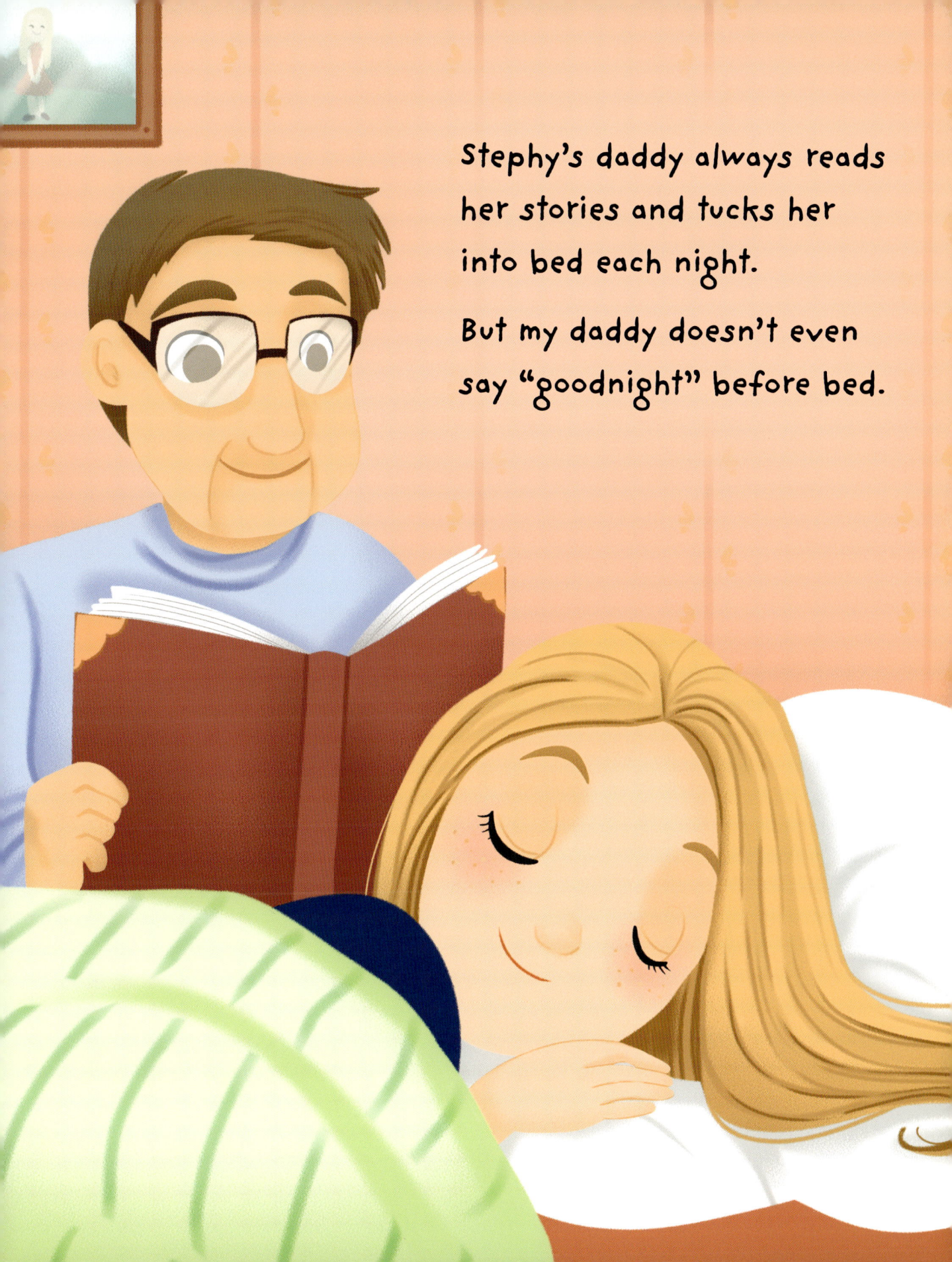

Stephy's daddy always reads her stories and tucks her into bed each night.

But my daddy doesn't even say "goodnight" before bed.

I thought he didn't love me, so I started to ignore him. When he came home from work, I didn't even bother to say, "Hi." When he apologized for not being able to come to my soccer games, I just shrugged. "Whatever. I don't need you there anyway."

But these days, I'm starting to think
DADDY MIGHT ACTUALLY LOVE ME.

Last week, at 5:30 in the morning, he was clomping around the house getting ready for work. I was annoyed because his shuffling had woken me up.

The next thing I knew, Daddy had snuck into my room.

He picked up my blanket that had fallen on the floor and draped it over me. Then he planted a light kiss on my head.

I hadn't expected that.

The next night, I had a terrible nightmare. I woke up and tiptoed down to my parents' room, planning to sleep with them for the night.

Right when I was about to open their door, I heard them whispering.

"Honey, I couldn't bear to look at the disappointment on her face," Daddy said. "I wanted to buy her all the board games and dolls that she picked up at the store, but I just couldn't."

"It's okay," Mommy replied. "You're working to give us a house to live in and food to eat."

"I barely even spend time with her," Daddy continued. "What kind of a dad am I?"

At that moment, I heard him sniffle.

I was confused.

A house to live in? Food to eat?

Then it all made sense to me!

Daddy earns money by working long hours. With that money, he makes sure our family has a home to live in and food to eat.

It wasn't that Daddy didn't care about me. He did—he just didn't show it like other daddies do.

I leaned in closer and the door let out a CREAK!

I scurried back to my room and jumped back into bed. *Phew, that was close!* I thought.

That night, I slept knowing that I have a daddy who cares about me.

The nightmare wasn't even on my mind anymore.

The next morning, I found a letter on the side of my bed.

> Dear Sumi,
>
> Daddy loves you so much —more than I show. I'm sorry I can't be there for you and give you everything you want. I will try to make more time for us from now on.
>
> Love,
> Daddy

Now it was my time to sniffle.

MY DADDY LOVES ME.

It may be hard to see that at first.

He may not show it in the ways my friends' daddies do, but he loves me in his own ways.

One day, I'll share my secret with him: that I, too, love him very much.

Sarah and JoAnn Jung are sisters currently living in New Jersey. This is their first time publishing a book, and they had a blast writing a story together. They hope that the young readers will grow in their appreciation for their dads or dad-like figures who may not seem "perfect" but do their best to show that they love their children.

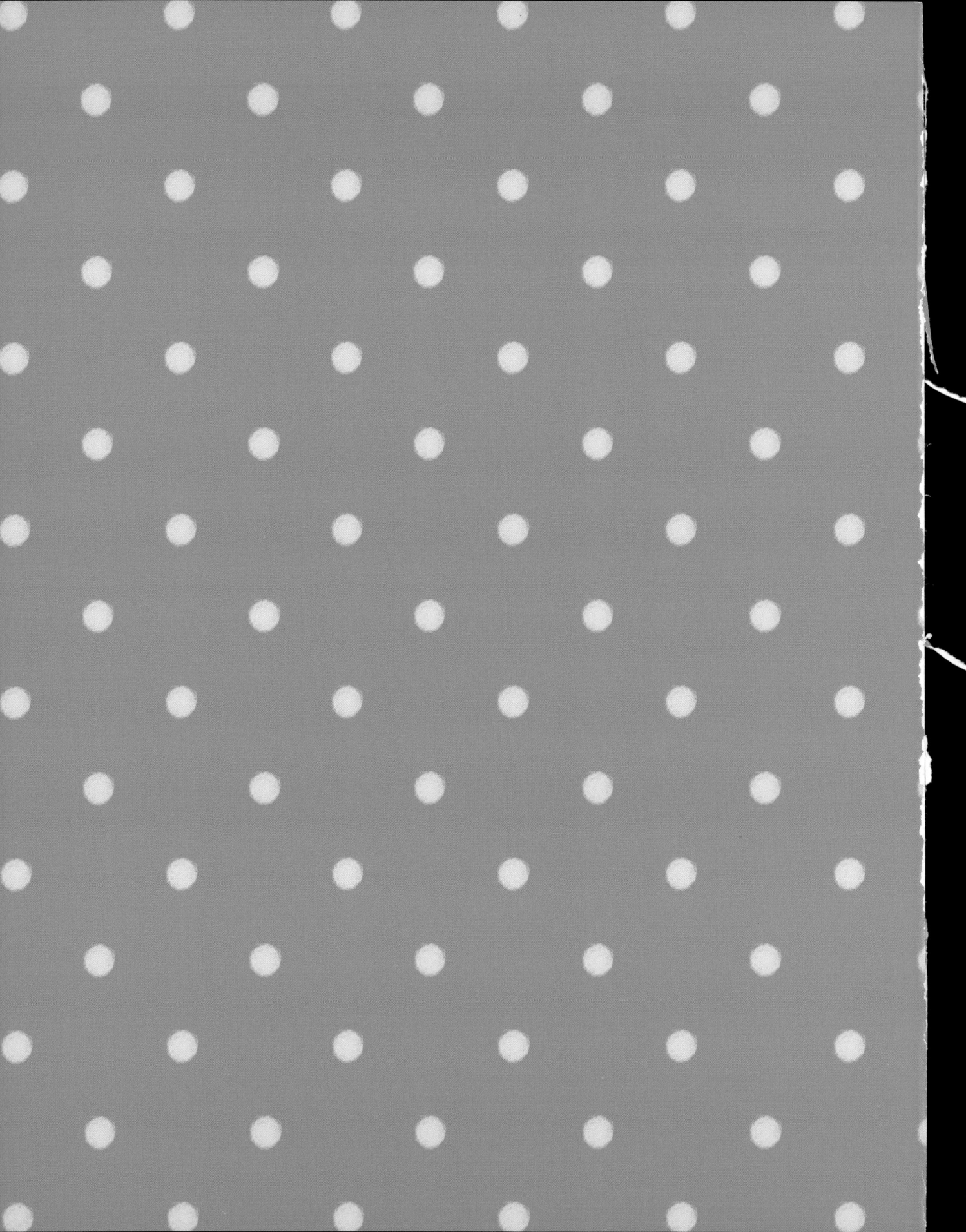